the
people,

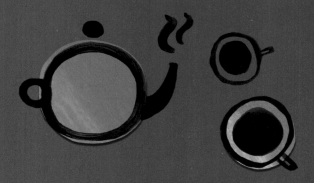
the
tea cups,

even the
**sprinkles on
the cookies**

Fitting In

Haruka Aoki and John Olson

Sky Pony Press
New York

In the land of circles,
no matter where you looked,
everything was round.

This book belongs to:

In one house lived two circles
who loved each other very much
and wanted to start a family.

But when their dream finally
came true, something was different.
Their baby was a square!

What would the other circles say?

A special gift
arrived for little Square's
first birthday.

Square's parents were thrilled.

"Now you can look like all the other circles!"

At school, all
the circles bopped
and boogied.

But even with the
extra shapes, Square
still felt different.

The circles would
leap and laugh,
run and roll . . .

But Square never
seemed to fit in.

At night, Square would come
home and take off the extra shapes.
What a relief it was!

When Square
fell asleep, all kinds
of shapes danced
and played together.

But when the sun
rose, Square woke up
from the dream . . .

and put on the extra
shapes, ready for another
lonely day at school.

Each year,
the circles had
a big, beautiful
party.

"I'll take pictures of the cute couples!"
"I hope they play my favorite song. *Toot toot!*"
"I'm going to wear my new suit!"

Everyone seemed excited but Square.

Will I fit in at the party? Square thought.

"You'll have a lovely time!"
Square's parents promised.

Maybe they're right. It could be fun!
Square straightened the extra shapes
and got ready for the party.

There were
circles, circles
everywhere!

One circle took a suprised
Square by the hand.

"Come join
the dance!"

Square leapt
into the air
for a twirl...

but tripped and tumbled to the floor.

All of Square's extra shapes had fallen off!

One circle
walked up to Square.
"Don't cry . . ."

"I'm not a
circle either.
I'm a triangle!"

"I'm a diamond!"

"I'm a star!"

"And I'm a rectangle!"

"We were scared, too. . . .
But thanks to you, we don't
have to hide anymore."

For the first time, it felt great to be a square!

Pointy, squiggly,
flat, or round . . .

The differences
were what made each
shape so special.

For the gentle, quieter souls out there.
You're not alone. — Haruka

For Adler. — John

Copyright © 2022 by Haruka Aoki and John Olson

All rights reserved. No part of this book may be reproduced in any manner without the express written consent of the publisher, except in the case of brief excerpts in critical reviews or articles. All inquiries should be addressed to Sky Pony Press, 307 West 36th Street, 11th Floor, New York, NY 10018.

Sky Pony Press books may be purchased in bulk at special discounts for sales promotion, corporate gifts, fund-raising, or educational purposes. Special editions can also be created to specifications. For details, contact the Special Sales Department, Sky Pony Press, 307 West 36th Street, 11th Floor, New York, NY 10018 or info@skyhorsepublishing.com.

Sky Pony® is a registered trademark of Skyhorse Publishing, Inc.®, a Delaware corporation.

Visit our website at www.skyponypress.com.

10 9 8 7 6 5 4 3 2 1

Library of Congress Cataloging-in-Publication Data

Names: Aoki, Haruka, author. | Olson, John, author.
Title: Fitting in : an inclusive story celebrating what makes you unique! /
Haruka Aoki and John Olson.
Description: New York, NY : Sky Pony Press, [2022] | Audience: Ages 3–8. |
Audience: Grades K-1. | Summary: Square tries to find into a world of circles by pretending to be one,
until an unexpected event makes Square learn to celebrate being different.
Identifiers: LCCN 2022005288 (print) | LCCN 2022005289 (ebook) | ISBN 9781510772106 (hardcover) | ISBN 9781510773523 (epub)
Subjects: CYAC: Individuality–Fiction. | Shape–Fiction. | LCGFT: Picture books.
Classification: LCC PZ7.1.A637 Fi 2022 (print) | LCC PZ7.1.A637 (ebook) | DDC [E]–dc23
LC record available at https://lccn.loc.gov/2022005288
LC ebook record available at https://lccn.loc.gov/2022005289

Cover design and artwork by Haruka Aoki and John Olson

Print ISBN: 978-1-5107-7210-6
Ebook ISBN: 978-1-5107-7352-3

Printed in China

WITHDRAWN
Anne Arundel Co Library